CAN YOU SURVIVE AN

ALIEN INVASION?

An Interactive Doomsday Adventure

by *BLAKE HOENA*
illustrated by *PAUL FISHER*

raintree

a Capstone company — publishers for children

Raintree is an imprint of Capstone Global Library Limited, a company incorporated in England and Wales having its registered office at 7 Pilgrim Street, London, EC4V 6LB – Registered company number: 6695582

www.raintree.co.uk
myorders@raintree.co.uk

Text © Capstone Global Library Limited 2016
The moral rights of the proprietor have been asserted.

Editorial Credits
Anthony Wacholtz, editor; Bobbie Nuytten, designer; Wanda Winch, media researcher; Kathy McColley, production specialist; Nathan Gassman, creative director

ISBN 978 1 4747 0708 4
19 18 17 16 15
10 9 8 7 6 5 4 3 2 1

British Library Cataloguing in Publication Data
A full catalogue record for this book is available from the British Library.

Acknowledgements
Shutterstock: CS Stock, (background, throughout), Nevada31, 106, Stefano Garau, 100, Stocksnapper, 103, Ursatii, 104

Every effort has been made to contact copyright holders of material reproduced in this book. Any omissions will be rectified in subsequent printings if notice is given to the publisher.

All the Internet addresses (URLs) given in this book were valid at the time of going to press. However, due to the dynamic nature of the Internet, some addresses may have changed, or sites may have changed or ceased to exist since publication. While the author and publisher regret any inconvenience this may cause readers, no responsibility for any such changes can be accepted by either the author or the publisher.

Printed in China.

CONTENTS

ABOUT YOUR
ADVENTURE

You are living through a dark and dangerous time in the near future of humanity. An advanced alien race has invaded Earth, their purpose yet unknown. How will you survive? Start off by turning the page, then follow the directions at the bottom of each page. The choices you make will change the outcome of your story. When you have finished your path, go back and read the others to see how other choices would have changed your fate. Do you have what it takes to survive doomsday?

YOU CHOOSE the path you take through an Alien Invasion.

ALIEN INVASION!

The distant city is surrounded in a hazy glow. With all its bright lights the stars are barely visible from the rooftop of your block of flats. That's why you're standing out in the middle of a field on a school night – to get a clear view of the sky. Thousands of brilliant points of light dot the darkness above.

Your best friend, Jacob, was supposed to be here with you. You are working on an astronomy project together. He said he'd meet you just after sunset, but that was an hour ago.

You glance at your phone. He hasn't returned any of your texts. Worry fills your thoughts. *Have his parents grounded him? Has he crashed his bike?*

You can't let Jacob's absence stop you. You have to be home in a couple of hours, and you need to make some observations to complete your project.

Turn the page

You just wish Jacob was here to help. You had to lug your gear all the way from the side of the road, where you left your bike, to a clearing in the field. That was after the 8-kilometre bike ride to get here, which wasn't easy with your telescope strapped to your back. But at least everything is set up now.

Your telescope has an 80mm refractor lens and, on a clear night, you can see the rings of Saturn. Tonight, you're actually hoping to chart a couple of Saturn's larger moons. That should earn you an A for your project.

You check your phone again. Nothing.

Where is Jacob?

You will have to start without him. You turn to your telescope and spot Saturn low in the sky. It's a bright unblinking dot amongst the dimmer, twinkling stars. You aim your telescope in its direction and bend over to look through the eyepiece.

After fiddling with the controls for a moment, you bring the planet into focus. Saturn's rings have a 3D effect, making the planet look like it's just hanging there in front of you.

Suddenly, a flash of light fills the lens and blinds you. You stagger backwards.

What was that? you wonder, as you rub the fuzziness from your eyes. *A meteor?*

But when your vision clears, you are amazed at how wrong you are. Hovering high up in the sky is a large bluish light surrounded by several smaller swirling lights. They are all too big to be planets or stars and moving around too randomly to be satellites. One swoops down near the ground and then shoots back up to rejoin the others. Another darts ahead of the rest, only to regroup a second later.

Your imagination can come up with only one answer for what they might be. It's a thought that both frightens and excites you: *UFOs!*

Turn the page

That has to be it. Nothing else could move like this. Not weather balloons or aeroplanes, birds or insects.

Your heart begins to race. If only Jacob were here, you'd have someone to back up your story. No one's going to believe that you saw a UFO.

You start to turn your telescope towards the lights that you suspect are alien craft. You want to get a better look at them, but they quickly scatter. Only the largest of the lights holds its place in the sky. You wonder if it's the mother ship.

One of the smaller lights settles behind some trees along the edge of the field. Having an alien spaceship land so close frightens you. It could be dangerous, but curiosity is urging you to investigate.

To investigate the UFO, turn to page 12.
To get away from the UFO, turn to page 16.

This is an opportunity you can't miss out on. You have to see what the aliens look like. And you have to take a few photos – proof for those people who won't believe you actually saw a UFO.

You grab the bag lying next to your telescope. Inside is a torch with red film taped over the end of the lens. You turn it on, and it glows red. It's a trick you learned in a science lesson at school. Red light does not affect your night vision.

The alien ship is in the opposite direction from your bike, but you don't care – even if it means staying out late and possibly getting into trouble. Your parents will understand when they see the photos.

You jog across the field, keeping your torch aimed low at the ground so you can avoid any ruts in the field. You have to slow down when you get to the trees. Branches swat at your face and arms. Roots threaten to trip up your feet.

You creep through the undergrowth as quietly as you can. When you near the edge of the foliage, you stop and duck behind a tree. Peeking out from behind its trunk, you spot a disc-shaped craft in a clearing. It hovers a couple of metres above the ground. A sphere of blue light shines from the bottom and crackles with the hum of energy. The ship is small. It can't be more than 6 metres in diameter and is probably 2 metres high.

It might be a scout ship, you think.

Turn the page

You want to sneak closer to get a better look. But then a hatch opens in the bottom of the craft. You duck back behind the tree.

What descends from the opening isn't a little green man – it's a robot. The robot stands about waist high and is shaped like a large drink can. It hovers just centimetres above the ground on a smaller version of the blue energy orb that seems to power the spacecraft.

Several aerials stick out from the robot's body. They whirl and jerk about as they scan the area. Arms with clawed hands extend from panels on the robot. The hands reach down to pick up rocks, leaves, twigs – anything they can find. The items are then deposited in an opening at the top of the robot. It looks as though it's gathering samples, but why?

To take a picture of the UFO, turn to page 18.
To try to make contact with the aliens, turn to page 21.

You've never really believed in aliens because the people who tell stories about them always seem a bit odd. But now that you've seen a UFO, you don't want to risk being poked and prodded by little green men. So you pack up your telescope and the rest of your stuff. You sling the bag over your shoulder. Then you hunch down, and as quickly as you can, you jog towards your bike.

Despite the possible danger, you wish you'd taken some photos. It would be good to have proof that you'd seen a UFO. You're pretty sure if you mention anything to your friends, they'll tease you about it and say you've gone mad.

You glance back, curious to see where the alien ship is. To your surprise, it's now hovering over the clearing where you had set up your telescope. A green beam of light shines down from the ship. The light whirls around on the ground as if scanning for something.

Do they know I'm out here? you wonder.

Then the green light stops on something for just a moment before it starts combing over the ground you have just crossed. The ship slowly moves in your direction. You start to worry that the aliens know you're here, and you wonder about their intentions. Are they friendly or not?

You've read plenty of stories about alien encounters. Some people black out. They may wake up hours or even days later not realizing any time has passed. Many of them can't recall what happened to them. You instinctively look down at your phone, to check the day and time, just in case. Then you turn to run.

In the distance, you see a pair of headlights cutting through the night. A car speeds down the road towards you.

To run for your bike, turn to page 23.
To try to stop the car, turn to page 24.

As you lean around the tree, you pull your phone from your back pocket. The spaceship looms over the clearing. There are no windows or visible hatches on its surface, except the opening through which the robot descended. You can't tell if anyone is looking back at you, or even if there are aliens flying the ship.

The robot continues to gather samples. As it gets closer to your hiding spot, you focus the phone's camera on it. You hear a soft click, and there's a bright flash as your phone snaps a picture.

The robot immediately stops. All of its aerials click and whirl in your direction.

Uh-oh!

From the bottom of the UFO, a green light beams down on the ground. The beam whips from side to side across the clearing as if it's searching for something. Any plants caught in the light begin to wilt. You watch in horror as the beam makes its way towards you.

Turn the page

Another robot descends from the opening in the spaceship. This one looks different from the first – more menacing. It's almost bullet-shaped, with a red glowing light on top. It immediately begins to follow the green beam of light, which is closing in on you.

You worry that you will be spotted if you move from behind the tree. But as the beam nears your hiding spot, a wave of nausea washes over you. You feel like throwing up or passing out. All around you, leaves turn brown and start to shrivel.

Then the robot reaches the edge of the clearing. From a panel in its side, an arm extends with a whirling blade. It starts buzzing through the foliage.

Fear grips you, and you turn to run away.

A beam of red light erupts from behind you. You feel the heat of the blast as it barely misses you, scorching the ground ahead.

You run for your life.

Turn to page 27.

You've read all the strange and frightening stories about alien abductions – none of which you believe. The people behind those stories always seem a bit odd. You'd probably be the first normal person to see and meet an alien. People would believe you. You're sure of it.

Unless meeting the aliens is what made those other people odd, you wonder.

Still, you want to have solid proof of this meeting, so you pull out your phone. You bring up a video app and start recording as you step from your hiding spot.

You are watching the screen of your phone and not where you are walking. As you enter the clearing, a twig snaps underfoot. Suddenly, all of the robot's aerials snap in your direction. It beeps and buzzes at you as its arms retract into their panels.

Turn the page

"Um, hi," you say nervously, not knowing whether the robot will actually understand you. "I won't hurt you."

The alien robot doesn't move, so you take another step forward. Then another. You cautiously approach as the robot continues to click and beep at you. Not wanting to miss anything, you continue to record what's happening.

You are close enough to reach out and touch the robot when a green beam of light shoots down from the bottom of the UFO behind it. The light quickly whirls around on the ground. You watch in amazement as plants shrivel up in its wake. Then the light washes over you. Nausea grips your stomach. As you double over, your legs give out. You drop your phone and collapse to the ground. The last thing you remember is rising up from the ground and floating towards an opening in the bottom of the ship.

Turn to page 30.

In the stories you've read about alien encounters, cars stall and lose power. You let your telescope slide from your shoulder, knowing you'll be faster without it. You run off in the direction of your bike, which is hidden behind a hedge along the side of the road.

Meanwhile, the alien craft veers towards the approaching car. The vehicle's lights flicker, and the car stalls in the middle of the road. The UFO's green light washes over the car. The passenger door opens, and an unconscious woman collapses to the ground.

Then a panel opens in the bottom of the spaceship. As if by magic, the woman is lifted off the ground. She begins to float towards the opening of the ship. While you would like to see what happens next, this is your chance to get away.

Realizing you'd be easily seen on the road, you leave your bike behind and head out on foot instead. There is a grove about 50 metres from you. You run for cover as fast as your legs will carry you.

Turn to page 27.

You want to get away, and in a hurry. So you dart into the middle of the road and wave your arms frantically. The approaching car's headlights blind you and, for a second, you aren't sure the car is going to stop.

A horn blares. Tyres screech. You shut your eyes tight. Then silence. The car has skidded to a halt just metres away from you.

You run to the passenger side. A young woman rolls down the window.

"Is something wrong?" she asks.

The man driving yells, "You nearly got yourself killed!"

You point at the approaching alien ship.

"Is that a…" the woman's voice trails off as she turns pale.

"Get in!" the man shouts. You immediately jump into the back seat.

Turn the page

As the UFO gets closer, the car's tyres squeal. You race ahead with the UFO in pursuit. You look out the rear window, watching in horror as the alien ship easily catches up with you. It positions itself directly over the car. The headlights flicker. The engine splutters and stalls.

"Derek, do something!" the young woman shouts.

The driver hopelessly cranks on the ignition. "It won't start!"

We have to run, you think. But before you can get the words out, the green light shines down on the car. A wave of nausea washes over you.

"I'm going to be sick," the man says as he opens his car door.

You open your door as well, but your legs won't work. You fall out, unconscious.

Turn to page 30.

You run through the trees as branches swat at your face and scratch your arms. Your side hurts, and your lungs burn as you suck in air. But fear propels you forward. What you saw back there scared you more than you've ever been scared before. And no matter what, you know that you don't want to be caught under the alien ship's green light. Who knows what will happen to you then.

You're not sure how long you've been running. You glance back to see if you're being followed. The UFO isn't in sight. Everything is dark behind you.

Maybe it's safe, you think. *At least for now.*

You slow your pace to a fast walk so that you can catch your breath. You pull your phone out of your back pocket. You have to tell someone what has just happened.

Turn the page

Wow! Look at all these texts from Jacob.

You start to read them:

You there?

You won't believe what I just saw. A UFO!

Seriously. I'm not crazy.

That's why he was late. Perhaps he saw the same alien ships that you saw.

You start shooting back replies:

I know. I saw them too.

Stay away from the green light!

You stop for a moment to wait for a response.

None.

Then you notice that Jacob's last text was sent about an hour ago. That's before you even saw the aliens.

Did they get him? You worry.

As you continue to scroll through the rest of his texts, your screen goes blank.

What's happened? you wonder. *Have I lost reception?*

You tap the message icon several times. Nothing pops up. You hold your phone up in the air, but that doesn't help either. As you look up, you see hundreds of flares exploding high above you. It's like a fireworks display across the whole night sky.

Satellites? That's when you realize what's happening: *The aliens are destroying Earth's communication satellites. That's why my phone went dead.*

As if on cue, you see a green light flash behind you. The alien ship is flying just above the trees and speeding in your direction. You need to find a place to hide. Somewhere that will protect you from the UFO's green light.

Near you is a thick clump of undergrowth. Further ahead, you see a farmhouse with some lights on.

To hide in the undergrowth, turn to page 33.
To run for the farmhouse, turn to page 38.

When you wake up, a bright light shines down, blinding you. You turn away, finding yourself face to face with a robot. Only, it doesn't have a face – just many arms. Some end in needles and scalpels. Others end in aerials and things with functions you can't even imagine.

You try to kick your legs, but they are strapped down. You want to push the robot away, but your arms are bound. So you do the only thing you can do – you scream at the top of your voice.

"HELP! HELP! HELP!"

The robot doesn't even flinch. It keeps going about its business, probably knowing that there is no one who will hear you.

From a panel in the side of the robot, an arm pops out with a light at the end of it. The arm starts to whirl about, and light forms a circle in front of you.

Turn the page

31

Then the robot buzzes three times. You stop your screaming to listen.

Maybe it's trying to communicate, you think.

There's a pause before the robot emits another buzz. Then four quick buzzes. And then one more buzz before it pauses again.

But this time, the robot waits for a few moments, as if it's expecting a response. All the while, its spinning arm continues to circle around and around, creating a perfect ring of light above you. You think the robot is watching you as its aerials click and whirl in your direction.

Then the robot repeats the pattern. Three buzzes. Pause. One buzz. Four buzzes. One buzz.

What does it mean? you wonder. *Is it a code, like Morse code?*

If you know what the buzzes mean, turn to page 35.
If you don't know what they mean, turn to page 65.

You've seen how fast the alien ships can fly. You've watched them dart across the sky. So you worry that the farmhouse is too far away. You might not make it in time, and there's a chance you won't be able to get in, even if you do make it. Your only hope is to hide.

You jump into the undergrowth, suffering several cuts and scrapes as you burrow deep into the foliage. Once the leaves and branches block out the night sky, you stop and wait.

The ship hums loudly as it approaches. Green light fills the area and even reaches you in your hiding place. You start to feel sick as you watch the leaves shrivel around you. You feel like throwing up and passing out all at the same time, and you curl up into a ball.

Then, a moment later, you hear the buzz of the ship zipping by. You wait a bit longer before daring to crawl out of your hiding place.

Turn the page

As you untangle yourself from the undergrowth, you spot a robot approaching. It is bullet-shaped with a glowing red light on top. The robot hovers a few centimetres above the ground on a blue ball of energy, similar to the UFO. It stands about waist high and has several aerials sticking out of side panels. They whirl about, scanning the area.

You think of ducking back into the undergrowth, but the robot's aerials twitch in your direction. You've been spotted.

Then the top of the robot begins to glow bright red. You turn to run, but it's too late. A red burst lights up the night, and you collapse to the ground, dead.

THE END
To follow another path, turn to page 10.
To learn more about aliens, turn to page 101.

"3.141," you whisper. "That's the first four digits of pi." That's what the buzzes represent. And the circle of light – you need pi to work out the area or circumference of a circle.

Your recognition prompts a series of clicks and ticks from the robot. Its arm stops spinning the light and retracts into the side panel. Then you watch helplessly as other arms connect a wire to your forehead.

Your mind is instantly flooded with images. First a distant view of a green and blue Earth. Then fighter planes being zapped out of the air by alien spacecraft. Tanks exploding. A green light washing over soldiers, who instantly collapse.

You realize you're seeing visions of the fighting that's happening all over the world. It's an invasion, and the aliens are trying to show you how badly the war is going for humans.

Turn the page

Then the images turn away from the fighting, but are equally as destructive. They show huge spacecraft flying over swaths of fields and forests. The ships harvest everything in their paths: plants, trees, animals. They leave behind barren soil.

They want food. That's why the aliens have invaded.

The last images are of alien ships leaving behind a less green world, but at least leaving the planet intact. The message is clear, and now you know the aliens' purpose.

The robot starts to unstrap your restraints. Behind it, a door slides open.

To try to escape, turn to page 42.
To go peacefully, turn to page 44.

There are lights on in the farmhouse, so you hope someone's at home. Perhaps they know what's going on. At the very least, maybe they can help you hide.

You sprint to the front door and give it several loud bangs. A second later, the door creaks open just enough for a pair of eyes to look out. It's a girl about your age.

"Wh-who is it?" You can tell she's terrified.

"Quick, let me in, " you shout. "There are aliens after me!"

"So what they're saying on TV is real?" she asks. "Not like that H.G. Wells thing?"

"They're real," you reply. "And they're here."

The girl's eyes widen. You turn around and see the alien ship fast approaching.

"Quick," she says. "Come inside."

She lets you in, then slams the door shut, locking it. Just inside stand two young boys. They stare at you wide-eyed. Behind them is a static-filled TV screen.

"I'm babysitting, and I'm responsible for these boys," she says nervously. "What should we do?"

"Is there somewhere to hide?" you ask. "A basement?"

She nods. Grabbing the boys by their arms, she leads you to a door, which opens on to a set of stairs.

"It's a storage cellar."

She's about to flick on the light when you stop her.

"They might see us," you say.

In the dark, you creep down the stairs behind the girl and boys. There are a couple of narrow windows, and you see the ground outside is awash with green light. The edge of the ship hovers over the house.

Turn the page

"Over here," the girl whispers.

There are several shelves full of camping gear. You see sleeping bags and a small axe, plus pots, cool boxes, and fishing rods.

"I'm going to be sick," one of the boys says.

You can feel it too. The green light from the alien ship is getting stronger. Being in the basement of the house isn't shielding you from its effect.

"They must be just outside the house," you say.

"Do you think they'll try to get in?" the girl asks.

To hide in the camping gear, turn to page 48.
To defend yourself against the aliens, turn to page 49.

As soon as you're free from your restraints, you kick at the robot, knocking it backwards. Its aerials whirl and buzz as the robot beeps and buzzes loudly. Claw hands shoot from panels on its side. They reach and snap for you, but you're too quick. In an instant, you're on your feet and running.

You dart out the door, but you don't know where to go. You just hope that at some point you find a way out. The ship didn't seem that big when you first saw it, so there has to be a way out somewhere near by. But then a scary thought crosses your mind, *What if I'm not in one of the smaller ships, but the mother ship?*

You don't let that thought stop you. The corridors are narrow and low. You have to hunch over to get through them. Maybe the aliens really *are* little green men. But then you think back to the short robot in the examination room, and you understand that these passageways are designed for robots.

Are there actually any aliens? you wonder. So far you've only seen robots. But right now, that's the least of your worries. You need to find a way off of this spaceship, and the corridor you dashed down doesn't give you much hope of that. The walls are as smooth as glass. There are no seams or handles. No windows to see out of either. Nothing that gives a hint of a door or escape hatch.

So you keep running down what feels like an endless corridor. And that makes you worry. You must be on a larger ship than the one that captured you.

The first opening you come across leads to the right – towards the centre of the ship.

To go through the doorway, turn to page 51.
To keep running, turn to page 56.

As soon as your restraints are loosened, you sit up. The robot reaches out with a clawed hand and grabs your wrist. If you want to escape, it's too late now. You could never pull away from its vice-like grip. Then the robot leads you from the room.

You are led along a short, narrow corridor. You have to duck as you go because the ceiling is so low. Either the aliens are little green men, or this passageway was built for the robots. That makes you wonder, *are there any aliens aboard this ship?*

The robot stops in front of a blank wall. It clicks a couple times. A panel opens to reveal a room. You are pushed through the opening, and the panel slides shut. You feel around the wall, but you can't find a seam where the opening was.

"It's no use," a familiar voice says behind you.

You turn, surprised to see your friend Jacob. Dozens of people stand behind him looking frightened. They look dirty and ragged compared to the clean, smooth walls surrounding them.

Turn the page

"I've already tried," Jacob says.

"So there's no way out?"

He shakes his head. You verify his answer by looking around the room. There are no doors, windows or vents. Just blank walls. You're discouraged, but at least you've found your friend.

"I was about a kilometre from the field when I saw a blue light behind some trees," Jacob says. "I stopped to see what it was, and that's when I saw the UFO. I tried texting you, but it didn't seem like they were getting through."

You look around again before asking the question that most worries you, "What do you think they're going to do with us?"

"I have no idea," Jacob says.

You're not sure how long you are locked up in the room. It could be minutes or hours. Time seems stuck within these blank walls. Every now and then, another person is pushed through the doorway that suddenly appears and then disappears.

Just when you think the room can't take any more people a door slides open in the far wall.

Two robots enter the room. They have metal rods that emit a green light. When they wave a rod towards you, you feel sick. Using the rods, the aliens force all of you to move.

You leave the spaceship, happy to be on solid ground again. You're forced into a large holding pen with what seems like thousands of people. No one knows what will happen next or how long you will have to wait here. You simply know that the aliens will eventually leave. You just worry what the planet will be like when they do.

THE END

To follow another path, turn to page 10.
To learn more about aliens, turn to page 101.

You quickly unroll the sleeping bags and clear some space on the lowest shelf. You tell the boys and their babysitter to crawl under the shelf. Then you cover them with the sleeping bags.

There is also a Mylar blanket in what looks like an outdoor survival kit. You pull it over you and crouch down, ducking into the bottom shelf.

All of a sudden, the sick feeling goes away.

Have the aliens left?

You peek through an opening in the blanket. Everything is still lit up in green light. You look over to the girl and boys. Their sleeping bags are sprawled out on the floor, as if they've passed out. You realize the Mylar blanket must be protecting you.

You hear something bump against the front door upstairs. Then there's the sound of splintering wood.

The floor creaks above you.

To go and fight, turn to page 59.
To stay hidden, turn to page 75.

You grab some sleeping bags and hand them to the girl.

"Hide under these," you say.

"What are you going to do?" the girl asks.

"I'm not really sure," you say as you grab the axe. "But maybe I can stop them getting to you and the boys."

Slowly, you creep upstairs. With each step, you feel more and more sick. The effects of the green light are dizzying.

Then you hear the front door burst open. A humming sound enters the farmhouse and moves from room to room. You wait for it to come near the cellar door, trying not to vomit from the UFO's beam.

Then you throw the door open to find a robot. Aerials click and whirl in your direction.

Turn the page

You raise the axe to strike at the robot. But the effects of the green light are overwhelming. Your stomach wrenches, and you double over. Then your legs give out. You collapse, unconscious.

When you wake up, you are strapped to a table. A blinding light shines down on you, forcing you to look away. Hovering by you is a robot. Its arms end in needles, scalpels and other terrifying things.

The robot makes two beeping sounds. There's a pause before it makes three more beeps. Then five, then seven.

Are the beeps forming a pattern, like Morse code? Is it trying to communicate? The robot repeats the series of beeps one more time. Two. Three. Five. Seven.

If you know what the beeps mean, turn to page 63.
If you don't know what they mean, turn to page 65.

Going through the doorway seems as good an option as any. It opens into a large circular chamber. You are actually on the second level of the room, on a balcony looking down. Below you are several robots. They scurry about and fiddle with buttons and knobs along the room's walls.

You are amazed by what you see along the walls. The lower level of the room is covered with a bank of clear tubes filled with yellowish liquid. Inside each tube floats an alien. You can't see much of them. A tangle of wires is connected to their bodies, sticking out from their eyes, ears, mouths and chests.

Turn the page

As you stand there, a buzzing sound fills the air. Then all the robots leave the room.

They know I've escaped. They're looking for me.

Behind you, a panel slides over the doorway – you're now stuck in the room. There are no stairs or ladders to the main level, but the drop is only a couple of metres. You hang down from the balcony and then let yourself fall.

You quickly glance around to make sure there aren't any robots near by. The room is clear, so you walk up to the nearest alien-filled tube. It looks like they are asleep.

This must be how they stay alive during their long journeys through space.

Turn the page

But there is something else. As you examine one of the tubes, you notice that there are several small screens all around it. You touch one of them, and it flickers on.

What you see horrifies you. Several small alien ships hover over a factory. They send down red bolts of light that explode on impact. Chunks of debris fly everywhere as fires blaze. In the background, frightened people scream and run from the destruction.

This must be happening now, you think.

You touch another screen. This one shows the same scene, but from a different angle.

It's the view from a different ship.

You touch another screen, and you get yet another angle of the attack.

As you watch, you notice that the alien in the tube twitches and jerks slightly each time a blast is fired.

Then it dawns on you. You definitely aren't on one of the small scout ships. You must be on the mother ship, or at least a command ship. Possibly the larger blue light you saw earlier tonight. And this is the ship's command centre. Each of these aliens must be monitoring and directing an attack on Earth.

Thoughts whirl around in your head. *What should I do? What can I do?*

There must be some way to help the people who are being attacked.

As you stand there, unsure what to do next, a door panel slides open behind you. You turn to see a robot enter the room. It's similar to the one that was in the examination room.

When its aerials whip around towards you, it starts to beep and click. Then several metal arms pop out of panels in its body. Each one ends in a menacing clawed hand.

To try to escape, turn to page 68.
To attack the robot, turn to page 69.

You jog down the corridor as fast as you can. As you do, you run your hands along the walls. You hope to feel a seam where a door might be because you can't see any.

You worry that you are just running in a circle. But you haven't passed by the opening where the examination room was.

Suddenly, a door panel opens in front of you. Out pops a robot, only this one isn't like any you've seen so far. It has a more menacing look. It is bullet-shaped with a red glowing top.

An attack robot!

A beam of light bursts from the top of the robot. You duck as the beam shoots past you and scorches the wall.

Zzzzztt!

Turn the page

You turn and run back the way you came, hoping to get away. But then another beam of light grazes your shoulder, and you feel a burning pain.

Zzzzztt!

As you run, another panel opens to your right. A metallic hand reaches out and grabs your wrist. It's another one of the attack robots. You duck as it shoots a blast of light at you.

Zzzzztt!

With all your might, you try to pull your hand from its grip, but it's too strong. You're trapped. As you struggle, more robots come at you from both directions.

Zzzzztt!

You avoid the first blast, but the next one hits you in the chest. You slump over as your eyelids close.

THE END

To follow another path, turn to page 10.
To learn more about aliens, turn to page 101.

You hear the door leading to the basement open. Then a humming noise approaches. Peeking out from under the Mylar blanket, you see a blue light descending from above. It gets brighter as it gets closer. Then you see a metallic arm reach for the girl. She is dragged from her hiding place.

You can only hear what happens next. The whirl of the robot's arms. The sleeping bag falling to the ground. The robot must have picked her up. Then the blue light starts to move back upstairs.

You remember seeing an axe on the shelf with the rest of the camping gear. In one smooth motion, you stand – keeping the Mylar blanket wrapped around you – and grab the weapon.

Your movement attracts the attention of the robot. Its aerials turn, clicking and whirling in your direction.

Turn the page

But before the robot can act, you swing the axe as hard as you can.

Clang!

You put a dent in the top of the robot. You swing again and chop off an aerial.

Then arms shoot out from several openings in the robot's body. They end in clawed hands that snap and reach for you.

You hit one with the axe as it tears at your sweatshirt. Another reaches for your ankle, but you kick it away. All the while, you keep wildly swinging the axe. You chop off more aerials. Several of the robot's arms are limp and dangling.

You've also suffered several cuts and bruises. But when the robot drops the girl, you know you've won this fight.

The robot quickly retreats up the stairs and disappears through the doorway.

Turn the page

You drag the unconscious girl back to the shelves. You find a couple more Mylar blankets and cover her up. Then you spread blankets over the boys.

You're not sure how, but the Mylar blanket protected you from the aliens' green beam. It seemed to keep the robot from detecting you. So you hope the blankets will keep the girl and boys safe.

Then, from upstairs, you hear some loud buzzing. It sounds like more robots have entered the house. You need to get out and either lead the aliens away from the farmhouse or somehow distract them.

You check one of the basement's narrow windows and unhook the latch. It is just wide enough for you to crawl through. You are careful to make sure that you keep the Mylar blanket wrapped around you.

To find the alien craft, turn to page 72.
To make a run for it, turn to page 77.

Prime numbers! you think. *That's what the numbers are.*

You vaguely recall reading somewhere that maths is the universal language. Perhaps that's how the alien species is trying to communicate with humans.

Upon your recognition, the robot clicks and whirls. Then it unstraps you from the table. A claw hand shoots out and grabs your wrist in a vice-like grip. Any thoughts of escape leave your mind – there's no way you could pull away from the robot now.

The robot leads you down a short, narrow corridor. You have to duck as you go. At the end of the corridor, a door slides open. You are pushed through and enter a large room likean arena. It's filled with hundreds, or maybe thousands, of people. They all mill about, not sure what to do. You wonder if you know any of them.

Turn the page

A hand reaches out of the crowd and grabs your shoulder. You spin around. It's Jacob!

"Jacob! What happened to you?" you ask.

"I got zapped by one of their green lights and ended up here," he replies. "You?"

"Same," you say. "So what do they want?" You nod your head towards a bullet-shaped robot that is patrolling outside the pen.

"Food. At least, that's the rumour," Jacob says.

"They're going to eat us?" you ask worriedly.

"No," Jacob says. "Anyone who passes their intelligence test is safe as long as they don't fight back."

So, along with the rest of the prisoners, you wait. You wait for the aliens to take what they want from your planet. There is nothing else you can do, but you hope that Earth will be able to sustain the human race after the aliens leave.

THE END
To follow another path, turn to page 10.
To learn more about aliens, turn to page 101.

The alien robot pushes a button. All of a sudden, green light washes over you. You feel sick, like you're going to throw up or pass out. You kick and struggle against your restraints, but it's no use. Nausea overwhelms you, and you black out.

You wake up to the sound of mooing.

Is that a cow? you wonder.

Then you hear the grunt of a pig and the bleat of a sheep. For a brief moment, you think you're on a farm or in a dimly lit barn. But then the memories rush back to you. You remember the UFO, the robots and the green beam of light that knocked you out.

You sit up and see that you are in a large room. You can barely see the distant walls in the dim light. Cows, pigs and other farm animals roam freely about.

"He's awake," a voice says to your right.

You turn to see a group of people huddled together. You get up and walk over to them.

"Where are we?" you ask.

Turn the page

A sad-looking man turns to you and says, "The food pens, we think."

"What?" you ask, horrified.

"Yes," a woman adds. "We think the aliens invaded Earth to gather food."

In a way, that makes sense to you. Earth has metals and ores, but the aliens probably have plenty of those. But every living thing needs food and water to survive, and Earth has plenty of both.

"We think the robot was giving some sort of intelligence test," the man says. "I've seen them apply it to cats and squirrels. Anyone or anything that doesn't pass ends up here."

"So we're going to be food?" you ask, defeated.

The people just look at each other sadly and then hang their heads. Suddenly, the floor drops away from you, and you fall into darkness.

THE END

To follow another path, turn to page 10.
To learn more about aliens, turn to page 101.

You don't have any weapons. Your only option is to escape. As the robot lunges for you with its clinking hands, you dodge out of the way. Then you dart past it and head for the doorway.

But another robot fills the doorway before you can squeeze through. It reaches out with its metal hands and snags your sweatshirt. You hear a ripping sound as you pull away. Then more clawed hands reach out for your wrist, your thigh, your arm. There are too many too avoid. You're caught. As the robot's grip tightens, you scream in pain.

Then the other robot comes up behind you. Its claws dig into your side and neck. You continue to struggle, but you are helpless to defend yourself as a third robot attacks.

THE END
To follow another path, turn to page 10.
To learn more about aliens, turn to page 101.

The world is being devastated by aliens. But there must be something you can do. You're in one of their command ships. This is probably your best chance to stop them.

As the robot reaches for you, you duck away from its grasp and dart around it. Then you push it hard into the wall of screens. Sparks fly, and the robot jerks uncontrollably. Energy courses through it as one of its arms gets caught in some wiring.

The screen near you flickers and fizzles. You must have shorted some of them out. You wonder if that means the aliens can't see or control the spaceships that the screens are connected to.

Then you feel the ship shudder. You glance at the nearest alien. It's writhing in pain in its tube.

Maybe the aliens in the tubes are in control of this ship too, you think. *And maybe you can hurt them somehow.*

Turn the page

You have an idea. As another robot enters the room, you duck under its grasping arms. You shove it at one of the aliens in a tube.

To your surprise, the tube isn't made of glass or hard plastic – it's a clear, flexible material. As the robot rams into the tube, its outer surface bends inward. That's not what you were expecting. You had hoped the tube would shatter, spilling its contents on the floor.

But then the sharp edges of one of the robot's arms cuts through the tube. Yellow fluid starts leaking onto the floor. The alien shakes violently.

Alarms blare. Lights flash. More robots enter the room. But before they can attack you, the ship lurches. You and the robots crash into the wall. You feel a thunk on the back of your head, and everything goes black.

Turn to page 90.

As soon as you're through the window, you duck behind a hedge. Looking up, you can't see the alien ship. You think it may have landed in front of the house.

With your axe and Mylar blanket, you creep towards the corner of the house to peek around to the front garden. There, the UFO hovers a couple of metres off the ground. The robot you attacked is below the ship. Some of its arms and broken aerials are still dangling at its side. The robot is beeping and clicking loudly. *Probably communicating with the ship*, you think.

Then two bullet-shaped robots come out of the house to join the damaged robot. It doesn't look like they've found the girl and boys.

Suddenly, the green beam of light turns off, and the robots go silent. A hatch opens in the bottom of the ship. A figure descends from the hatch, floating on a blue metal disc. It's covered in a metallic suit and wearing a helmet. Slung over its back is a weapon.

A ray gun!

Turn the page

The alien approaches the damaged robot and looks it over. Then the alien glances at the two bullet-shaped robots, which have started to click and beep again.

The alien motions towards the front door. One of the robots darts through it as the alien follows. The other robot stations itself outside.

To protect the girl and boys, turn to page 81.
To capture the alien ship, turn to page 86.

You tuck the Mylar blanket tightly around you. Then you lean back under the shelving as far as you can.

The creaking upstairs moves throughout the house, then to the stairs leading down to the basement. You hear a humming noise approach. As it gets louder, a blue light fills the basement. You can see its glow through the blanket.

Then you hear some ruffling near you. It sounds as if the girl and boys are being dragged from their hiding places. But you don't dare move. You could get caught, too, or worse.

After a few moments, you hear the basement stairs creak. Then the blue light begins to fade.

When all is finally quiet in the house, you unwrap yourself from the blanket.

Turn the page

Next to you, the shelves are empty. The boys and girl are gone. They have been taken by the aliens.

To your surprise, the Mylar blanket not only protected you from the alien's green beam, but it also must have kept you from being detected. You doubt the aliens even knew you were there.

You feel guilty about letting the girl and boys get captured. But what could you have done?

Aliens have invaded the planet, and Earth's armies are destroyed. But in the coming days and weeks, what you've discovered about the Mylar blankets will prove to be important. After the initial attack, people begin to fight back, including you. And you could never have helped if you'd been captured. You just hope what you've learned is enough to survive the invasion.

THE END
To follow another path, turn to page 10.
To learn more about aliens, turn to page 101.

The alien ship has landed in front of the house, so you go around to the back of the house and head for the woods. You take cover behind some nearby trees and then run until you are out of breath.

You're not sure how far you make it before collapsing to the ground, exhausted. You are tired and afraid. You don't know what to do next.

As you sit there, you hear the crunch of approaching footsteps. You jump to your feet, ready to run away. But instead of a robot, you see a person step out from behind a tree. Then another. In all there are six people slowly creeping through the woods in your direction.

"Hey!" you shout.

They all stop.

"Keep it down," one of the people snaps.

Turn the page

Once the group has gathered around you, one of them asks, "Where did you come from?"

"And what's that you're wearing?" another man adds, pointing to the Mylar blanket. You tell them about spotting the UFO. Then you explain about the farmhouse and hiding from the aliens.

"You say that blanket protected you from the UFO's green beam?" one asks.

"Yes, and there are more in the farmhouse," you say. "But there's an alien ship there."

"A small one or a big one?" the man asks.

"I don't know," you say. "It's about 6 metres across."

"That's a small one," a woman says.

"It's not a command ship then," the man answers.

"No, those usually don't get too close to the surface," another person adds.

"So probably just a scout ship with a couple of attack robots," the man says. "We can take it." The people around him nod in agreement. *Turn the page*

You're surprised at their confidence, but as you look more closely at the group, you notice that many of the people have weapons. Rifles are strapped over their backs, and pistols are holstered at their sides.

"We've just started setting up a resistance in this area," the man explains. "Will you join us?"

You think back to the girl and the boys in the farmhouse. You feel guilty for leaving them there, and this will be an opportunity to see if they're safe.

"Yes," you say.

You join one of many small guerrilla groups that are fighting back against the aliens. You're told it could be a long fight, but the longer you survive, the better your odds are of defeating the aliens.

THE END
To follow another path, turn to page 10.
To learn more about aliens, turn to page 101.

The girl and the boys are still in the basement. You worry that they could be in danger with the alien in the house.

The front door is guarded by a robot, so you head back to the window. You crawl through it. You go over to the girl and boys. Now that the green light is off, they are stirring and starting to wake.

"Shhh," you say and point upstairs.

As if on cue, the floor creaks. The girl nods and pulls the boys to her.

With the axe poised to strike, you hide under the stairs. Then the door swings open. You hear the stairs creak. You see a metallic boot on the step above you. The alien slowly descends.

Turn the page

You come out and strike when you see the back of the alien's helmeted head. The axe cracks open the helmet. You get a whiff of foul-smelling air. The alien collapses to the ground, coughing and hacking, as if Earth's air is toxic to it.

You kick the alien over and take its weapon. Instead of a trigger, there's a place to put your hand in. When you grab it, the weapon wraps around your hand like a glove, as if it's now part of you.

From up the stairs, you hear clicking. You turn to see one of the attack robots at the top of the stairs. Its head is glowing bright red. You aim the weapon, but you don't know how to fire it.

I need to shoot, you think. As you think it, it happens. The ray gun fires, blasting a hole in the attack robot. From outside, you hear buzzing and beeping. The other robot appears at the top of the stairs, and you blast it, too.

Turn the page

Once you're sure that the danger is over, you turn to the alien. It lays lifeless on the floor. You're surprised that, in many ways, its face looks human, but with grey skin and large black eyes. It has eyebrows, a nose and a pair of thin lips.

You motion to the girl and boys to follow you. Then you creep up the stairs. There are no other aliens or robots around. You only wish you could call someone to tell them what you've done, what you've found. That there's an alien spacecraft sitting outside.

That's when you see it. A phone mounted to a wall.

"Do you still have a landline?" you ask the girl.

She nods. "Reception is rubbish out here."

You pick up the phone and dial 9-9-9.

"9-9-9 emergency. Which service do you require?"

"The police! I've just killed an alien!" you blurt out excitedly. You quickly retell your story.

"Help is on its way," the voice says, and then hangs up. Apparently, you're not the first person to call in about the alien invasion.

You turn to the girl, "Help is coming."

You realize that defeating the aliens will be a long fight. But you have a weapon that will add some firepower to your side.

THE END
To follow another path, turn to page 10.
To learn more about aliens, turn to page 101.

You are not sure which way the robot is facing – or if it even has a face. To play it safe, you pick up a stone and throw it to the far side of the garden, away from the ship. When it hits the ground, the robot's aerials go wild and whirl in the direction of the stone. The top of the robot starts to glow red with energy.

You pick up another stone and throw it further away and off to the side. The robot quickly heads in that direction. Then you make a dash for the spaceship.

The hatch on the bottom is still open, but there's no ladder. You leap up and grab hold of the rim of the hatch. As your feet kick wildly below, you feel a hot blast shoot past you.

The robot's seen me!

You quickly pull yourself up into the ship just as another blast shoots past you.

You crawl up inside the ship. The space you find yourself in isn't large, possibly 2 metres in diameter and only a metre high. It has a circular shape, with lights and panels covering the entire wall. In the centre is a chair.

Just then, you hear a buzzing sound from below. You glance through the hatch to see the attack robot. Its aerials are aimed in your direction. The top starts to glow red as you duck back into the ship's cockpit.

There's no escape now, so you only have one choice. You sit down in the chair.

What happens next both frightens and amazes you. Wires and tubes spring out of panels from the wall. Some wires embed themselves into the tips of your fingers while tubes latch onto your eyes.

Turn the page

Suddenly, instead of seeing what's around you, you're sensing what's around the ship. You hear the rustling of leaves. You feel the breeze flowing around you and even catch the smell of the night air. You're so amazed by it all that you almost forget where you are and what's happening.

Then the attack robot below the ship buzzes, catching your attention. It's signalling to the alien and other attack robot as they rush out of the house. The alien raises its weapon.

I have to defend myself, you think.

As the thought passes through your head, an energy field rises up around the ship. The field deflects the blast from the alien's weapon.

To attack the alien, turn to page 94.
To fly off, turn to page 96.

When you come round, your world is filled with smoke and sparks. You see a flashing screen and broken tubes. You try to stand, but you can't keep your balance. The floor is tilted at a drastic angle. The ship has crashed into Earth's surface!

All around you lies destruction. Yellow fluid is leaking out of the tubes. Alien bodies are sprawled on the floor. Some are dead. Others are gasping and coughing. You wonder if Earth's air is toxic to them.

You manage to untangle yourself from the wreckage. Then you crawl through the room's twisted doorway. You search the ship until you find an open hatch that leads out. As you crawl through it, a hand reaches for you from outside the ship and pulls you out.

Turn the page

As you're dragged from the wreckage, a voice asks, "How did you survive that crash?" You are pulled to your feet by a heavily armed man wearing camouflage.

"I don't know," you say as you shrug your shoulders. "Luck, I suppose."

"Come on, we need to get out of here," the man says. "They might come and see what happened to their command ship."

Debris is everywhere. Big chunks of metal cover the ground. The man leads you out of the wreckage and towards a cluster of trees. There a ragtag group of men and women are waiting. They are all armed and look at you with suspicion.

"Where did he come from?" a woman asks.

"I was inside the ship," you say. The man with you nods, as if to confirm your story. "I was fighting with some robots in its command centre when all this happened." You motion back towards the wreckage.

"You brought down a command ship?" a man asks, shocked.

"I've seen a fighter plane attack one of those ships and not leave a scratch," another says.

You see the suspicion in the soldiers' eyes turn to respect. Pride wells up in your chest.

"We need to tell the others what you found inside," says the man who helped you out of the wreckage.

You soon learn that these men and women are all part of an organized resistance. The next days and weeks are dangerous. You're constantly running and hiding from the aliens. But, so far, you are believed to be the only person who has seen what's inside an alien ship and escaped to tell the tale.

The information you have is crucial to the resistance. The soldiers you meet and talk to believe it will help defeat the aliens.

THE END

To follow another path, turn to page 10.
To learn more about aliens, turn to page 101.

The next thought that goes through your head is that you should attack. From the bottom of the ship, a red bolt of energy shoots forward. It disintegrates the alien and attack robot next to it.

I did that by just thinking it, you marvel.

You see the other attack robot fleeing towards some trees. You think of shooting it. Another energy bolt shoots from the spaceship and destroys the robot.

Excellent!

With the alien dead and the attack robots destroyed, you think of escaping. The spaceship lurches, almost, if it doesn't know where to go. You think "up," and it rises up. You're quickly hundreds of metres in the air. Even high off the ground, you can still sense everything around the ship. You see stars twinkling overhead.

Then you think "forward," and the ship races forward.

You are amazed at how easy it is to fly the spaceship, but you also wonder how you will disengage from all the wires and tubes connected to you.

In your mind, you keep hearing a series of clicks and whistles. You're not sure what they mean. You wish you could put your finger in your ear to stop the noise, but tubes cover them, and wires entangle your fingers.

Suddenly, the ship shudders, as though it's been hit by something.

Am I under attack?

Your senses pick up an approaching ship. It's not a small scout ship like the one you're in. It's an attack ship. It fires, and a wave of energy crackles over your ship. Your shields are knocked out.

Before you can think to flee, the attack ship fires again. Your ship explodes in a fiery ball.

THE END

To follow another path, turn to page 10.
To learn more about aliens, turn to page 101.

You are amazed that you have control of the alien ship and how easy it is to fly. You just think "up," and it shoots upwards. It's easier than using a video game controller.

The ship is only a small one, but you think it could definitely be useful. You could learn about the aliens' technology and maybe even find a way to fight back against the invaders. You just need to get it away from here, before more aliens come.

As if it's reading your mind, the ship lurches forwards a couple of metres.

Why won't it go?

You realize you need to think where you want it to go. In the distance, you see a thick grove.

I can hide the ship in there.

As you think it, the ship zooms forwards.

Turn the page

While you are flying, you hear some clicking and buzzing in your brain. There's a pattern to it, almost as if it were speech. You worry that the aliens are trying to communicate with the ship.

What will they do if they realize a human is flying it? you wonder.

Once you reach the trees, you set the ship down. You doubt you will be safe here for long, but you need a moment to work out what to do. Then you think about the ship powering down. Suddenly, the wires and tubes retract. You hope that shutting down the ship will prevent the aliens from tracking it.

You get out through the hatch and jump down to the ground. You're surprised to see several armed people surrounding you.

"Hey, he's not an alien," a woman says.

A man pokes you in the arm. "Are you human?"

"Yes! Don't shoot!" you shout, raising your hands in the air.

"Then you'd better explain yourself," the man says.

You quickly retell your story, starting with spotting the UFO and ending with the Mylar blankets and escaping with the ship. When you finish, the man in charge of the group tells you that they are setting up a resistance in this area. They are so impressed by your actions that they ask you to join them.

It will be a long fight to rid Earth of the invaders, but you have made a good start. You have one of their ships. Perhaps you can learn something about their technology that will help you fight back.

THE END

To follow another path, turn to page 10.
To learn more about aliens, turn to page 101.

LIFE AMONG THE STARS

Today, scientists are able to locate planets among the hundreds of billions of stars in our galaxy, the Milky Way. They can even estimate which planets are similar in size, possess water and circle a star similar to the Sun.

It is believed that billions of planets could be orbiting stars in what is known as the Goldilocks' zone. This area is close enough to a star to be warm but not too far away to be overly cold. This zone is believed to be perfect for the possibility of life. But because of their distance from Earth, we cannot determine whether life actually exists on any of these planets. However, that doesn't stop people from speculating that aliens exist, and have ventured to Earth.

Some people believe aliens have been visiting our planet for thousands of years. Some even think that alien technology helped build ancient marvels, from the pyramids to the giant statues on Easter Island.

It is hard to imagine how ancient civilizations had the ability to build these structures, so some people give aliens the credit. Most of these theories, however, have been debunked. Large sleds have been found in Egypt that were used to move the massive rocks that formed the pyramids. The statues on Easter Island are thought to have been brought there by boat – not alien ships.

The speculation that aliens have visited Earth often focuses on UFO sightings. Perhaps the most famous of these occurred in Roswell, New Mexico, USA. In July 1947, a rancher called William Brazel reported finding debris from a flying saucer. An officer from the local air base went to investigate. A few days later, a headline in the *Roswell Daily Record* read "RAAF Captures Flying Saucer on Ranch in Roswell Region." The military quickly denied this, stating that what was found was actually a weather balloon. But many wild tales sprang up about the events at Roswell. Some people even claim they saw alien bodies being recovered from the wreckage.

While reports of alien encounters can sound exciting, stories of alien abductions have also terrified people. One of the first reported abductions involved Barney and Betty Hill of New Hampshire, USA. On a night in September 1961, the couple was driving home when they saw what they claimed to be a UFO. Sometime later, the Hills discovered that their drive home took much longer than they realized – they were missing two hours of time.

Through hypnosis, the Hills recounted being stopped by aliens. They said they were taken aboard an alien craft and given medical examinations. But, so far, alien abductions have been as difficult to prove as alien encounters.

It's not hard to imagine the possibility of alien life somewhere among the stars. The universe is virtually limitless, so it's possible that there is life out there somewhere.

But none of the stories about alien encounters or abductions answer one key question: Why would aliens visit Earth? If you ask scientists, such as Stephen Hawking, it might be for conquest. Why else would they risk travelling billions of kilometres through space?

Just don't expect the aliens to be little green men. We send robots to explore distant planets. Aliens could do the same. The trip from their planet to ours might be too long and pose too many dangers for living creatures to survive.

We may never know if the stories about alien encounters and abductions hold any truth. Still, it's exciting to look up at the stars and wonder whether extraterrestrial beings live beyond our own solar system. And, if so, what their intentions towards Earth might be.

SURVIVAL GUIDE

In the unlikely event of an alien invasion, the key thing to remember is that alien technology would probably be more advanced than ours. If their ships can travel billions of kilometres through space, their weapons will be far more destructive as well.

But there is still hope. You just need to survive the initial onslaught. You'll need a survival kit that will help you in any situation:

SURVIVAL KIT

*Flint stone for making fire (waterproof matches will work too, but you may run out of them)

*Iodine tablets for making water safe to drink

*Swiss army knife

*First-aid kit

*Fishing rod, wlth line, hooks and sinkers

*Nylon rope, at least 8 metres

*Compass and map of area where you live

*Tarpaulin, to use for shelter

*Whistle, to use as an alarm in case of danger

*Mylar blanket, for warmth

*A warm, waterproof coat, gloves, scarf and hat

*Duct tape, for repairs

*Plastic bags, for storage

*Wire, at least 8 metres

*Cooking pots and eating utensils

*Hand-crank radio

*Torches, with spare batteries

*Walkie-talkies, with spare batteries

*Hiking shoes and an extra pair of warm clothes

*Stainless steel water bottle

*Bottled water (as much as you can carry)

*Non-perishable food (snack bars, instant soup and cereal)

TOP 10 SURVIVAL TIPS FOR AN ALIEN INVASION

- Any weapons you find probably won't match what the aliens possess. Your best defence is to hide.

- Get as far away from the alien forces as possible. Consider using underground tunnels and remote wilderness areas to hide in.

- Avoid populated areas. Large groups of people could attract the invaders' attention. There will also be more competition for resources, such as food and water, where masses of people gather.

- Avoid factories and military bases. These will probably be the first places that aliens attack in order to disable our ability to fight back.

- Avoid travelling on major roadways. They will most likely be blocked with traffic and debris.

- Make sure your hiding places have several different escape routes. Your first plan of escape might be blocked, so it's best to have more than one way to run from danger.

- It will be easier to survive in small groups than on your own. Keep your friends and family with you. You will be able to work together to find food, keep watch for each other and help one another should someone get hurt.

- Remember the three key things that you need to survive: shelter, food and water. Anything you bring with you must help obtain one of these essentials.

- You might not see any actual aliens during an alien invasion. If aliens attack, they might send robots because it would be difficult to survive the long trip to our planet. So don't just be on the lookout for little green creatures.

- The longer you survive, the better chance there is that the aliens will be defeated. Someone will either find a weakness in the aliens' technology or start a resistance to fight back against the invaders. The longer people can resist, the less likely the aliens will be willing to stay and fight, using up resources they need to return home.

GLOSSARY

ABDUCTION act of kidnapping, or taking someone against his or her will

ASTRONOMY study of stars, planets and other objects in space

DEBUNK disprove something

EXTRATERRESTRIAL life form that comes from outer space; extraterrestrial means "outside of Earth"

GUERRILLA warfare using small, surprise attacks rather than large battles

METEOR piece of rock or dust that enters Earth's atmosphere, causing a streak of light in the sky

MYLAR BLANKET blanket made of heat-reflective thin plastic sheeting; may be included in first-aid kits and camping equipment

NAUSEA feeling of sickness in the stomach that may cause vomiting

SATELLITE spacecraft used to send signals and information from one place to another

SPECULATION ideas or guesses about something that is unknown

READ MORE

Aliens and UFOs (Solving Mysteries with Science),
Lori Hile (Raintree, 2013)

Alien Storm (Superhumans), A.G. Taylor
(Usborne Publishing Ltd, 2010)

Amber, Julie Sykes (Curious Fox, 2013)

WEBSITES

**www.booktrust.org.uk/books/teenagers/writing-tips/
writing-fiction**
Have a go at writing your own alien invasion stories using
some of these top tips!

www.esa.int/esaKIDSen/
For real-life information about space and space
exploration, visit the European Space Agency website.

AUTHOR

Blake Hoena wrote his first story as a young child. It was about space aliens trying to steal the Moon. And ever since, he has been fascinated with little green men. He even created a graphic novel series about alien brothers, Eek and Ack, who try to conquer our blue planet. When not thinking about outer space, Blake writes children's books about mythology, skateboarding and poetry. He lives in Minnesota, USA, with his wife, two children and a couple of pets.

ILLUSTRATOR

Paul Fisher-Johnson graduated with a degree in Illustration from Swindon College's School of Art and Design. His work has been published more than 70 times and includes book covers, interior illustration and even greeting cards. Paul illustrates in both colour and black and white, and his special strength is figurative work. He lives near Bristol, with his three children, and spends his spare time writing music to perform with his band.